Francis Barnes, Royal Crafts Spaulding

Autobiogaphical Sketch of Rev. Royal Crafts Spaulding

And Extracts from Letters of Himself, and of His Wife

Francis Barnes, Royal Crafts Spaulding

Autobiogaphical Sketch of Rev. Royal Crafts Spaulding
And Extracts from Letters of Himself, and of His Wife

ISBN/EAN: 9783337135065

Printed in Europe, USA, Canada, Australia, Japan

Cover: Foto ©Raphael Reischuk / pixelio.de

More available books at **www.hansebooks.com**

ROYAL CRAFTS SPAULDING.

JERUSHA BRYANT SPAULDING.

We seek, not yours.
But you.

OF

Rev. Royal Crafts Spaulding,

AND

EXTRACTS FROM LETTERS OF HIMSELF,

AND OF HIS WIFE,

Jerusha Bryant Spaulding,

WITH NOTES AND EXPLANATORY TEXT.

ARRANGED AND EDITED BY

FRANCIS BARNES.

HOULTON, MAINE:
PRESS OF WILLIAM H. SMITH.
1891.

INTRODUCTORY.

In the evening of an August day of the year 1862, a young man who had been stopping at the Hotel in Houlton for a short time, asked the clerk where to find the house of Rev. R. C. Spaulding. The necessary information having been given, the stranger passed up the principal street of the village, till he reached the gateway of a double tenement, one story house, which he recognized as the indicated residence. The Western half was, to outward appearance, without inmates for the time being, for the windows were closed and the curtains all down except at one window in the back part of the house.

The caller rapped at the door, and waited some few moments for a response, but none came. At last, just as he was at the point of turning away, the front door was slowly opened and there presented herself to view a slight built, rather undersized, elderly woman, whose face was furrowed with wrinkles of age and care, but whose eyes shown with the undimmed energy of youth.

In a shrinking manner she inquired the stranger's wishes as though the sooner the errand were done the better. The caller had come for a purpose, and was not to be discouraged. He told his name, his purpose to settle in the place, and of his standing as a member of the Baptist Church. "Oh, I am so glad to see you!" she exclaimed, and extending her hand grasped the hand of the other most warmly. "We have just got home from one of our trips, and Mr. Spaulding is at the barn taking care of the horse. I had hardly got my things off." The caller said he would not intrude, but would call again.

Such was my first interview with the heroic wife, mother, and missionary, Jerusha Bryant Spaulding. To me it was a simple act of recognition of the fact of their residence in the place, and of their work, as I had read of them. Of any particular result I did not dream. To her it was "a gleam of light in a dark place," and in the quick flashing of her woman's intuition she saw the possibility for the Baptist Church of Houlton. As I learned afterwards, with the warm grasp of the hand there came to her mind the germ of the new and forward movement of the Baptist Cause, which for seventeen years her husband and herself had toiled, sacrificed, and waited for.

From that moment there began a warm friendship toward myself, on their part, and it continued till their death. They received me as they would their own son, and honored me with their most intimate confidences.

The association which circumstances thus brought about between us was of most lasting and powerful influence upon myself. They lived in the utmost exercise of faith; "the substance of things hoped for" was literally theirs. They had given themselves to God and His work. He would carry them through to the end.

Thus equipped with this most implicit, yet ardent faith, and fortified by a wise caution and an exhaustless patience they toiled and waited; "cast the bread beside all waters," in this great region, and, "after many days," the abundant harvest was before them.

It has been a labor of love to me, in these past few months, to collect, and arrange, as well as I could, the mementos of their priceless toil for souls. In this work I have been greatly aided by Mrs. Annie Spaulding Bradbury, of Milwaukee, Wisconsin, who surrendered to me the letters of her sainted parents, and also by the friends of the family in all the places where they lived. Truly "the memory of the just is blessed."

To all who have aided me so heartily I return most earnest thanks.

FRANCIS BARNES.

AUTOBIOGRAPHY.*

I was born in Plainfield, Sullivan Co., New Hampshire, July 29th, 1800. My parents, Joseph and Mary Elkins Spaulding, were of English descent and removed to Compton, Upper Canada, in my infancy, and lived there twelve years. In 1813 they moved back to the States, and resided in Pomfret, Connecticut.

I was awakened, when quite young, to a sense of my lost condition, but was nineteen years of age before I obtained a hope in Christ, and professed religion. I was then serving an apprenticeship at the saddle and harness-makers trade, in Pomfret, and was admitted to the Congregational Church in that place; but soon began, by reading of the New Testament, to be tried in my mind on the subject of baptism, and about one year from this time, having gone to Worcester, Massachusetts to work at my trade, I attended the meeting of Dr. Jonathan Going, and was baptized and united with the Baptist Church of which he was Pastor.

I now began to feel an ardent desire to become useful as a Christian, and supplied myself with some books to read and study for the improvement of my mind, which had been sadly neglected from my not having had the early advantages of a common school education. When my apprenticeship expired I went into my Pastor's family to get what help I could from reading and study, where I spent six months.

Then I worked my way along, and spent about six months in Rev. Mr. Fisher's school for young men which he taught in his own house in Bellingham, Mass. After that I attended two or three terms at Amherst Academy, and in 1824, by the advice and assistance of my good Pastor, Dr. Going, and the Church, I went to Waterville, and was there about two years, in the Theological Institute, attending to such branches as I most needed.

In 1826 the Officers of the College received a letter from Levant

*This sketch was prepared by Mr. Spaulding in the year 1876, after he was laid aside from his active labors, and was written at the request of Mr. E. P. Mayo, now Editor and Proprietor of the Fairfield Journal, but has never before been printed in full.

(now Kenduskeag) requesting them to send a student to spend his winter vacation in teaching their winter school, and preaching in their place on the Sabbath. There was no church of any Denomination in the town. I was advised by my teachers to go, and availed myself of the opportunity, expecting to return to Waterville again, when my school closed, to pursue my studies; but the leading men of the town, in their town meeting, chose a Committee of five to invite me to come and settle there as their minister, and were not willing for me to spend any more time at Waterville. After closing my school I went back, and made known to the Officers of the College the wishes of the people at Levant, and they thought it was a call which ought not be unheeded, and advised me by all means to comply. Though very reluctant to give up my regular studies I yielded to their advice, went back to Levant, and commenced my labors there for the people of the town. On the second day of May, 1826, I was ordained to the work of the Gospel Ministry; the meeting on the occasion being convened in a large, new barn, in the centre of the town. Dr. Chapin came from Waterville to preach the ordination sermon.*

In the summer of 1828, we had a small Baptist Church organized, and, on Oct. 7, same year, I was married to Miss Jerusha Barstow Bryant† of Bangor; so then I had a *Domestic* home, and an ecclesiastical home in the little town of Levant, and there we continued and labored until 1834. A small Congregational Church was organized, and they united with the Baptists in erecting a nice house of worship, in the village, to be occupied alternately by the Bap. and Cong. Societies. In Jan. 1834, I resigned my charge in Levant, and became Pastor of the Baptist Church at East Corinth, about six miles from Levant, where we labored nine years with that dear people, and formed precious friendship, in both of those towns, that we trust will be perpetuated in the heavenly world.

In the summer of 1844, I was sent by the Maine Baptist Missionary Board to Aroostook County, as one of the pioneer Missionaries;

---

*Rev. Otis Briggs of Hampden, and Mr. Dexter of Corinth aided in the services. (Memorial Discourse by Rev. Isaiah Record.)

†JERUSHA BARSTOW BRYANT was born at Newcastle, Lincoln Co., Maine, February 1, 1801. Her parents, Charles and Elizabeth Louden Bryant, were of Irish descent, and had a family of one son and eight daughters. When Jerusha was quite young the family removed to Bangor, where she became a constituent member of the First Baptist church, and lived until her marriage.

THE SPAULDING HOME.

SMITH PRINTS, HOULTON.

and the winter following, in the month of February, I moved my family* by the direction of the Mission Board to Houlton village, where we have remained for more than thirty years past; and what we have done, or left undone, we must leave altogether with Divine Providence, not without many regrets that we have accomplished so little.

Still I wish to acknowledge, with gratitude to God, that He has permitted us to work so long in His vineyard, and that He has been pleased, as I trust, to bless my poor labors with some success; and now I am laid aside from Zion's work, yet rejoice and thank God that His blessed cause is more and more precious to us both, and that we find His Holy Word a great comfort and support to us in our old age, with its infirmities.

Our earnest prayer shall continue, "Thy Kingdom come, Thy will be done in earth as it is in Heaven."

---

*Children of Royal Crafts and Jerusha Bryant Spaulding:

HENRY MARTYN, born at Levant, Maine, Nov. 15, 1829; died in Hackensack, N. J., April 22, 1880. Married Isabella Stephenson Mould, Aug. 20, 1867, at Lewisburg Penn. Henry served in the army during the war, enlisting from Ohio. He followed the profession of teaching up to the time of his death. He left a family of four children.

ANN JUDSON, born at Levant, Dec. 1, 1833; married James Tyler Bradbury, A. M. W. C. of Waterville, Me., Nov. 23, 1855. He died at West Liberty, W. Va., June 14, 1863.

Mrs. Bradbury has a family of three children, two sons and a daughter. She resides at Milwaukee, Wis.

HOWARD CLARKSON, born at Corinth, Me., Feb. 25, 1838; died at same place, Aug. 4, 1840.

BOARDMAN CAREY, born at Corinth, Me., Sept. 27, 1843; married Mary Ann McBrien of Houlton, Me., April 26, 1868. Boardman enlisted in the 17th Regt. U. S. Regular Army, in 1862, and was wounded at the battle of Chancellorsville. He was afterwards admitted to the Bar, in Aroostook County, Me., and moved to the West, nearly twenty years ago. His children are three sons and one daughter.

Under date of March 23, 1891, Mrs. Bradbury writes thus of that removal of the family:

"The most vivid impression of the long hard journey, in winter, from Bangor to Houlton, in a single sleigh, is snow and forest, forest and snow,—interminable, it seems; and the strange wild music of the winter wind in the tree-tops, and the sharp crackling of frosty limbs added to the dreary side of days — how many I do not know. Then there was a continued dread of meeting another team, as Mother with my baby-brother in her arms and I usually had to get out into the narrow road, while the men held up the sleigh as the horse plunged through the deep snow. My little brother, sixteen month old, must be carefully covered from the intense cold, as he lay in Mother's arms, and carefully watched lest he be smothered.

On arrival at Houlton, February 1, 1845, Mother's birthday, we went to Mr. Hussey's tavern, standing with its front to the West, where now stands the B. H. Putnam block; and then came the reaction after the terrible ride, and my Mother had a severe illness. After her recovery we moved into the house, which my Father bought in 1851, the only one we ever lived in, in Houlton.

The Garrison was seeing its best days then,— the stars and stripes always flying from the tall flag-staff, and sunrise and sunset regularly registered by the morning and evening gun. There came a time when the little village was made sad, as the troops marched down through town and away in response to the summons to Mexico."

"What we have done,"
And the manner of it.

CORINTH.*

GLENBURN, MAINE, NOV. 6, 1890.

DEAR SIR :

I read the notice in the *Advocate* of your purpose to prepare a memorial of Mr. and Mrs. Spaulding. I am glad this work is to be done.

Mr. Spaulding was settled in Corinth, my native place, for nine years, and among my earliest and pleasantest recollections are those of the visits which he and his wife made, at my Father's house. Father, Mother, and children were always delighted to see them. I remember well how he used to come in and shake hands with every one of the family; and we, very little children, all felt that he had a personal interest in us. Then his gentleness and gentlemanliness won us. I recall both his and Mrs. Spaulding's manner, as though it were but yesterday. What unaffected sympathy, and what warm Christian love beamed from their countenances and dropped from their lips!

I was not more than eight years old, when they left Corinth for the Aroostook, yet so strongly had their beautiful Christian lives impressed my mind that time does not efface, but rather deepens the feeling. It was a great grief to my parents, and their family, when Mr. Spaulding felt called to leave us; but his own spirit of self-sacrifice had been measurably imparted to them, and they were led to acquiesce, feeling that the hand of God was in it.

Both husband and wife possessed large faith; they were ad-

---

*The first letter is from Mrs. Abbie Jones Goodwin, and the second from her sister, Mrs. Charlotte Jones Merwin, now resident in Conn. Their Father's name was George W. Jones, a farmer of Corinth, Me., and an earnest member of the Baptist Church.

A portion of a letter from Mrs. Spaulding to their Mother follows.

vanced thinkers; indeed, were almost prophets, and they were, at Corinth, "in labors more abundant."

The parish was a large one, but every part was carefully and frequently visited. They made all the people interested in Missions: the *Macedonian* was thoroughly distributed among the members, and there was always the monthly concert of prayer, with collection for missions. Every Sunday evening, in the meeting house, at five o'clock, or, in winter, "at early candlelight," was held the prayer meeting, and, on Tuesday and Thursday evenings, social meetings were held in the houses, among the neighbors. Mrs. Spaulding instituted the maternal, or female prayer meeting, and its sessions were regularly held and the attendance large.

Besides these stated occasions, Mr. Spaulding very frequently had preaching appointments in the outlying district. The Sunday School was held between the preaching services, followed by the choosing of books from the well-filled Library. Many of the books was the gift of Mr. Spaulding. Their nine years of seed sowing, in Corinth, laid the foundations of the Church strong, symmetrical, and sure. These memories are as of yesterday to me, deepened too by subsequent meetings with them, when they had come down, in their wagon, over the long road, to attend the yearly sessions of the Penobscot Association. The pleasure of going to the Association was always enhanced to my parents by the prospect of meeting their old pastor and his wife; and as often as possible they secured a brief visit from them. To our family they were just the same; we could see no change except "a going on unto perfection."

New Haven, Feb. 6, 1891.

Dear Sister:

I enclose a letter of Mrs. Spaulding's to Mother. I think she must have sent it to me to read. I can testify to the worth of those faithful servants of God. Their devoted piety and consistent living impressed me, when a child, of the reality of religion. I think Corinth has a great deal to thank Mr. and Mrs. Spaulding for. They worked for the elevation, as well as salvation of the people, and practiced what they preached. They tried to arouse a missionary interest by books and papers, and would go without their own tea and coffee to give to the cause. They strove to in-

terest the young, and procured a library of excellent books, all
covered, numbered, and catalogued, which proved a great help to
both old and young.

They were ready for every good work, earnest, devoted, faithful,
sparing not themselves; "living examples known and read of all
men," and "their works do follow them."

HOULTON, March 17. 1864.

MY DEAR SISTER JONES:

How time flies! Your interesting letter ought to have been
answered long ago,—but if you knew *half* the things that hinder
my writing I know you would willingly excuse me. We both feel
very grateful to you for writing to us, and telling us so much about
our dear Corinth friends, whose welfare is always interesting to us
and will be, as long as we live. * * * How I should like a
photograph album with all the pictures of our dear old friends of
Corinth and young friends too! Dea. Hunting* gave us his like-
ness, last Fall, when we were there, and we can hardly look at it,
since you told us of his death, without bringing the tears to our
eyes,—not tears of sorrow, because he has gone to join the re-
deemed family above, but of tender recollections of the many
offices of kindness that we received from him, during our residence
in that favored place; and of his earnest, untiring labors for the
good of the Church and the cause of Christ. * * * I would
be glad to write to your dear daughter, if I only had time, but
our labors are more abundant than usual, this winter, having sick
ones to visit and funerals to attend, in several towns around; besides all our regular meetings in different places, our children's
correspondence to attend to, and our household concerns to keep
in order.

---

*Deacon John Hunting was a miller by trade, and proprietor of Hunting's Mills. He
was one of the strong men of that strong church, and died shortly before this letter was
written.

THE MISSIONARY SUMMER.

HOULTON, July 16, 1844.

MY DEAR WIFE:

I stayed at Bro. Robinson's, the night after I left home; left there early, took breakfast with Bro. Staples, dined at Oldtown, and spent that night at Enfield. Friday, I drove fifty-four miles, and stayed at the Forks. Saturday, drove twenty-four miles, and stayed at Sister Ingersol's in Houlton. I preached twice on the Sabbath, two miles out of the village, shall have two lectures, this week, and preach in Linneus next Sabbath. Dined, to-day, with Sister Tupper, wife of widow Tupper's son. He belongs to the Cong. church; she is a very decided Baptist. She is the daughter of Deacon Noah Smith of Calais, and writes for *The Mother's Assistant* and *The Young Lady's Friend.* Her name was Ellen S. Smith. Her Father and Mother taught the first Sabbath school, in the United States, in the City of Providence. Three times he has seen his whole class converted and united with the church.

This Sister Tupper has two Sabbath schools in this place, one in the morning, at the Cong. Meeting House, of thirty scholars, which she has collected from the streets herself, and another, about three miles distant from the first, at four o'clock P. M., at the place where I preached, last Sabbath.

The Baptist Church in this place exists only in name. When I arrived here, there was no appointment made. In the morning I had twenty, in the afternoon, some more than thirty. They had received my letter, but did not know what to do as they have no head nor anything else; yet I hope to do some good, if Christians pray and the Lord blesses.

When I become settled I will tell you more about my situation. * * * Remember me affectionately to Brother John, tell him there is a great field of labor here.

Your husband, very sincerely and affectionately,

R. C. SPAULDING.

BELFAST ACADEMY GRANT, July 31, 1844.

MY DEARLY BELOVED WIFE AND CHILDREN:

This is the third day that it has rained, and I do not go out much. I am at the house of Gen. Cummings,* the uncle of Isaac and Rebecca Cummings of Bangor. They are very kind, hospitable people. He and his wife and son's wife are Baptist professors. This place is seven miles from Houlton. I preached here, last Sabbath, to a small, crowded school-house. Two men and their wives came from Limerick, round through Houlton, twelve miles.

The next day after I wrote to you last, I preached a lecture, two miles North of Houlton village; on the next day preached again at Hodgdon, five miles South of H. Saturday I went to Linneus, ten miles on the road toward Bangor, and stayed at the house of Bro. Nickerson.† The children were all at home. In the evening, Edward and his wife came in and we had a prayer meeting. In the morning we went to the school-house where Elizabeth teaches, four miles, and I preached to more than a house full. Sister N. rode with us, and carried a little baby four or five weeks old. Went back to Bro. N.'s house, and stayed all night. Next morning he handed me a five dollar bill and wished me to let him have some books for it.

I then returned to Houlton; stayed at Sister Hussey's. Her husband is an innkeeper, not a professor but a very kind and pleasant man. He told me to make it my home when I wished. Tuesday afternoon, I came to this place. Wednesday morning, I left my horse at Gen. C's and, walking about a mile and a half, I called at every house. Then I went one mile, North, through the

---

*John Cummings came to the plantation of New Limerick, some little time prior to the year, 1830. He had been living at Winthrop, Kennebec Co., and owed his title of General to position in the State Militia.

By deed of Aug. 23d, 1830, the Trustees of Belfast Academy conveyed to him several lots of land in their Grant, which lay just North of the Limerick Grant.

He soon moved his family to the Belfast land, and lived there till the time of his death. He was the first settler on the Grant, and a man of influence through the communities about.

†Thomas Nickerson with his wife and quite a large family of children, moved from Charleston, Penobscot Co. to Linneus, in March, 1842. He bought out some person who had begun an improvement on the lot, and received his deed from the Proprietor, John Hodgdon, in the Fall of 1843. Mr. Nickerson had the title of Colonel from Militia service, and was acquainted with Mr. Spaulding and his family while the latter was settled in Corinth. Col. Nickerson was a pleasant and hospitable man in his home, and the minister was always a welcome guest. He was a strong supporter of the Baptist cause during his active life.

woods to Bro. Gilman's, asked them for some bread and milk which was very nice, and had a good rest. After talking and praying with the family, I gave them a bible and some tracts. I left them and went back to the road again. South of this town is Limerick, and all that separates it from Belfast is a piece of woods, about three and a half miles wide. We cannot go through with a carriage. I then entered the woods by a foot-path, and, finding a log house, called and gave some tracts. I asked how far it was to the next house and was told, three miles. I went on, but found it very hard and slow walking. I got there about night, found a very interesting and respectable family and stayed that night; appointed a lecture there the next day, at five o'clock. Next morning visited and gave notice of the meeting. Some more than twenty present at the meeting; two women came five miles. I spoke of God's condescending love to His people.

Friday morning, went back towards Belfast. Took another path, worse than the first, that I might call upon some other families, got through the woods about noon; to this place where I now am, about four, and at five o'clock, preached a lecture in the school-house close by. I tried to show weak and doubting Christians that the word and promises of God will never fail. One sickly but pious woman walked more than two miles. She came from the house where I gave the bible.

Saturday morning, I thought I would rest for the Sabbath. But I looked toward Houlton, (for where I am now writing, in my chamber, I can see Houlton village, seven miles East of us, and on a hill beyond it the Garrison, in full view. It looks like another small village; and a little from that I can see the Parish of Richmond, in the British Province,) and I so longed for a letter that I got my horse and went down. Called at the Office and, to my joy, I found one. I knew the handwriting, I walked very fast to my room. When I opened the letter and saw how full it was I laughed out aloud. I began to read it, and sometimes I would laugh and cry together. I thank you a thousand times for your *good letter*. After I read it I tried to pray for you all. I kissed the letter and also little B. C.'s marks. In the afternoon, I came back to this place where I preached, last Sabbath, as I before said.

Next Sabbath, I preach in Limerick. The people are poor in these towns. In this, the children have no schools of any kind to attend. Our dear favored children do not know anything of poverty and want. I want the children to learn as fast as they can. I want to know how fast they are getting along. Is Ann's Botany the right edition? Ask Mr. Thurston; show it to him and if it is not, ask him to get one for her. Ask for the tuition bill, before the term expires, and show it to Bro. Brownson. I want you to have some coal. Mr. Goodwin can tell you where to get some, six cents a bushel. I want you to get some ripe currants. Let H. and Ann go some where and pick you some; carry the money and offer to pay for them. You need them for your health, I want you to have some fresh lamb or beef. Ask Mr. Norcross who has it to sell. I will pay for it when I come home. It will grieve me to think that you are doing without anything that you need. I want the children to write *longer* letters, and you to write *no shorter* ones.

Saturday morning, Houlton, Aug. 3: To-morrow I preach in Linneus. There are no prayer meetings among the Baptists, in any of the towns, where I go to preach, I am trying to arrange for some female prayer meetings. Next week I hope to have some commenced, one in Belfast and another in Houlton. I wish you would write a *circular letter* to the Baptist sisters, in Linneus, in Belfast, in Limerick, and Houlton. I think it would do good. I feel a deep and growing interest in this region. I want the children to get an *education* and come and *instruct schools.*

I long to see you all, but I must be patient. I am willing to stay here, if I can do good to my fellow-men, and also be earning something to educate my dear children. I look toward Charleston very often. If I could fly I would be there, once a week. My health is *very good.*

Yours, most affectionately,
R. C. SPAULDING.

P. S.—*Sat. night.* This afternoon, we have appointed a female prayer meeting, at Sister Tupper's, for next Friday, at two o'clock. R. C. S.

HOULTON, Aug. 27, 1844.

MY DEARLY BELOVED WIFE:

I have just returned to Houlton, after an absence of a week.

during which time I visited Hodgdon, Belfast, Smyrna, and the Foxcroft settlement, and preached five sermons.

The interest of our meetings, I think increases * * * The Sabbath that it rained and you went to meeting, only half a day, I preached in Limerick, and Bro. Nickerson and his wife came from Linneus, thirteen miles, and brought a babe, seven weeks old.

God blessed that day to one man, who had not spoken of religion, or prayed in secret, for thirteen years; he commenced praying in his family, that night. Next Sabbath after, I preached at Linneus, with a very full house, had a third service in a school-house near Bro. N.'s; he confessed and wept, and four of his children did the same. We went from this place to his house, and had a prayer meeting, himself and four of his sons prayed.

We have begun regular prayer meetings at his house, for each Tuesday evening. Two persons rose for prayers during the day time.

Next Sabbath, I preach, two miles out of the village, in Houlton. Last Sabbath, in Belfast, then came back, seven miles, to tea; then three miles further, to an early service, at Foxcroft, where I preached, in the house of a Mr. Keen.

Next Sabbath, which will be the first day of Sept., I shall preach, also, in Houlton village, in a new school-house, just finished, near the Unitarian Meeting House. We have had no place here before; hereafter I shall preach half the time, in *this place*, so you will know when I preach in Houlton, as it will be once in two weeks. I have been here seven Sabbaths, and I have only eight more to stay; then I do hope to see my dear wife and children again.

Elder Kendall has been here and called at the places, where I have preached; and he told me that I was very well received, and he wanted to engage me to spend the winter here. He says the Society would be glad to appoint me, and that it would be best to remove my family here; but I shall do as my wife and children think best about it. I want you to attend the Association at Bangor. * * *

Your sincere and affectionate husband,

R. C. SPAULDING.

P. S. Please direct the letter which you will write to the Sisters to me, in Houlton; write a whole sheet. There is an interesting female prayer meeting in Belfast, and in Houlton.

R. C. S.

The next letter is from Sister Spaulding to her husband, and evidently crossed the preceding one, as it was on its way. The letter is a most interesting one, as it gives evidence of the full development of the spirit of self-denial and consecration which so strongly marked all her subsequent life. It cost something of a struggle to turn from a call to Boston to the woods of the North-east.

CHARLESTON, ME., Aug. 30, 1844.

MY DEAR HUSBAND:

Bro. Nickerson has just called to see us, and has given me a few moments to write, while he calls upon Mr. Thurston; and now I do not know what to say first, my mind is so confused in hearing from you so suddenly. We have been looking very anxiously for a letter from you, and began to have some fears that you were sick, because no letter came, this week; and when Henry Martyn saw Mr. Nickerson ride up to the door he was somewhat alarmed, and came running in saying that Mr. Nickerson had come, and he was afraid he had come to tell us that Pa was dead; but we soon had our minds relieved by hearing that you were well when he left home.

We begin now to count the weeks with more courage than we did when you went away. The children inquired, this morning, how many weeks longer Pa would stay. I told them he would stay four weeks after next Wednesday. They thought they should be glad when they could count days instead of weeks.

Bro. N. thinks you would consent to stay four weeks longer, if it was thought best. I suppose he meant, if the Missionary Society would continue to employ you. I am glad to hear that you feel so much interest, and encouragement in your labors, but, my dear husband, I hope you will not forget the *Boston folks.* I am afraid they will feel very badly, if they do not hear from you, at the end of three months, as that is the time you asked them to wait.

Bro. N. wishes to know if *I* am willing to go and live in that region. I answer, "Yes, I am willing to go anywhere, if I can do any good."

Mr. Thurston's bill for last term is paid; it was just six dollars.

The fall term* commences next Monday. We are expecting a very full school; there will be no school, at Corinth, before next Spring, and quite a number are coming up from there, this Fall. Henry Dexter and Gideon Smith called on me last week. They came to engage houseroom for Gideon and Lydia Ann, and Oreb and Almira Dexter. Bro. Jackson and wife, and Bro. Haines and wife, were up, last week, and made me a good visit.

Bro. N. has just come back, and I must close. O how I want to see you! My heart says, "Come home as soon as you can," but my Missionary spirit says, "Stay as long as you agreed to."

We all join in much love.

Yours, most affectionately,

J. SPAULDING.

---

*of the Charleston Academy which, after a long and honorable career, has recently become the Higgins Classical Institute, under the control and oversight of Colby University.

IN LABORS ABUNDANT.

MY VERY DEAR DAUGHTER:

In my last I told you I was going to Hodgdon, and would write you from there. So here I am,—it is just one week this evening since we came here. I am now sitting at the little stand by the sitting room fire. Mrs. Bradbury sits at my left hand in the large arm chair reading the *Macedonian*, which was brought up from the Post Office, a little while ago. Dea. Bradbury has gone to the Club meeting this evening, * * * and Boardy is capering round in the kitchen with the cat and dog, I suppose, by the noise he is making.

We are all in usual health and comfortable circumstances. Don't you wish you were here with us? We do; but trusting in a kind Preserver that you are well we will not murmer because you are not with us. Our Quarterly Meeting commenced Friday evening, and, after spending two days and evenings in session, our meetings were so interesting that we concluded to continue them evenings for a while, so we have met every evening since, till this evening the Temperance folks occupy the house and we have a meeting appointed for tomorrow evening. The church members* are considerably revived in their minds, and we think there are some indications of a revival of religion. O, pray for

---

*"The Calvinist Baptist Church of Hodgdon and Number 10" was organized on Jan. 15, 1835, at a meeting of those friendly to such a movement, which was held in the Yellow School-house, so-called, the first building for such a purpose erected in the town. It stood on the County Road, about three and one-half miles from Houlton village.

There were present for the services, besides the people of the town, Rev. Elisha Bedell of Deer Island, Rev. Gilbert Spurr of Brighton, Rev. Lothrop Hammond of Prince William,

us that it may be even so! We have had no ministers but Pa and Mr. Emerson.† Last evening Mr. Emerson preached, and thirteen of the church members spoke after the sermon.

To-day, Pa has gone to the Lake, where he spends the Sabbath, and I stay here to attend the meetings and visit the Hodgdon folks a little. I have not been on the hill yet but expect to before I go home. We have had very favorable weather and good sleighing since our meetings began, but it looks now very much like rain.

We all join together here in wishing you "happy New Year."

Ever, your affectionate Mother.

Dea. J. Foster of Douglas, and Bro. Abraham Newcomb of Richmond, all of the Province of New Brunswick except Mr. Bedell.

Rev. Mr. Spurr was chosen Moderator, and Rev. Mr. Bedell, Clerk. Fourteen men and fifteen women were found ready to unite themselves together in the bonds of church fellowship. It was voted to proceed with the organization of the church. James Johnson and J. N. Foster were chosen Deacons, and Howard P. Towne, Clerk.

The young church soon widened its field of activity, and with Rev. E. Bedell as Pastor, began to gather in recruits in other towns and plantations.

During the next spring Columbus Dunn of No. 10 experienced religion, and joining the church was elected an additional Deacon on May 30, of same year.

Of the constituent members of this Mother Church of all the Baptist Churches of this section only two now survive: Sarah Ann Towne, youngest child of Ebenezer and Mary Pettingill Towne, born at Maugerville, N. B., Dec. 5, 1815; came with her parents to Hodgdon in 1825, and was converted in a revival among the Free Will Baptists, who held meetings in the house of Dr. Chesley Drew, in the Spring of 1830; she married Daniel Outhouse April 19, 1833, and he died in Ludlow, Me., Oct. 8, 1878; also, Mrs. Rebecca Snow Dunn, wife of Columbus Dunn of Number 10. Sister Dunn was born in Orrington, Me., in the year 1808, was married in 1827, and moved immediately to their home, now the town of Amity.

She was converted in the meetings held by Mr. Bedell, in the early part of the winter of 1834-35, and was baptised by him, with others, in the Eastern part of the town of Hodgdon. Dea. Dunn died suddenly in November, 1878.

Deacon Bradbury, alluded to in the first lines of the letter, was Christopher Columbus Bradbury, originally of Limerick, York Co., Me., who with his brother, True Bradbury and Jonathan Hayes of the same town bought the legislative Grant made to the Limerick Academy. This tract became known as New Limerick, and Mr. Spaulding refers to it, at times, as merely Limerick. Prior to this purchase Christopher had gone to Prince William, York Co., N. B., to work at his trade of wool carder and cloth-dresser.

There he married Miss Mary Joscelyn, and they had one child, James Tyler Bradbury, subsequently the husband of Annie Spaulding.

In 1828 he moved to the New Limerick Plantation, and in 1835, with a cousin, Jabez Bradbury, he bought the mill privilege in Hodgdon and made that place his home. May 12, 1838, Mr. Bradbury and his wife were received to the church, and on May 30, they were baptised by Rev. Thomas Murray, at that time, Pastor of the church. Bro. Bradbury was chosen and ordained Deacon, Feb. 17, 1839.

James Tyler Bradbury was received into the church March 2, 1843, and was chosen Clerk.

June 7, 1846, was the first baptism administered by Bro. Spaulding. Aug. 29, of same year, Mr. and Mrs. Spaulding joined the Hodgdon Church.

Aug. 17, 1857, Dea. Bradbury and his wife were dismissed to join the Baptist Church in Waterville, where they had gone to live with their son.

†Mr. Emerson was a Congregational Minister, who lived at Springfield, Penobscot Co., and was on a visit to his friends in Houlton and Hodgdon.

Houlton, Feb. 1, 1855.

My Dearest Daughter:

We received your letter, Tuesday evening, requesting us to send your book of Sketches. We took it from the Post Office as we returned from Limerick, where we had been four days. Pa preached there, last Sabbath, in the day time, and out to Mr. Berry's in the evening. We spent the night there, and the next morning, Mr. Berry invited us in to his store and gave me a nice calico dress-pattern, (I wish you could run home and make it for me) and a capital pair of shoes, and some other things. We visited all day, Monday and Tuesday, in Limerick, and I was so tired when we got home that I had to rest all day yesterday—that is, I could'nt do anything but my housework. I wanted to write to you and send your book this morning, but I had'nt courage enough to touch a pen. To-day I have done a large *wash*, and feel better this evening, so I will try and get a short letter ready to mail for you to-morrow evening with the book.

We rejoice that your health continues good, and we hope it will be so that you can stay and take lessons another term; tell us all about it when you write again.* Hannah and Angelia are making all preparations to go to Auburndale; they expect to go in a fortnight, I believe. Perhaps they will call on you. Clara Ingersol is spending her vacation with her Aunt Louisa in Dorchester.

Boardy stayed with Mrs. Pierce while we were gone to Limerick; she will not let him go away if she can help it. He carried his melodeon in there and played for them, a number of times, each day, and they carried it up to the Meeting House, Sunday, and he played for them, in the forenoon and afternoon. Mrs. Pierce told me that he played beautifully, and they sung so well that she felt perfectly satisfied. Mrs. Ingersol called upon us yesterday,—she said the melodeon sounded so sweetly that it made her cry. * * *

Do you know *this* is my birthday? Yes, I have lived in this world fifty-four years. It is but a short space of time, and yet it seems a great while to me. Long before the same number of

---

*The letters of this chapter are all by Mrs. Spaulding to her daughter, Ann Judson, who had gone to Waterville to study music. In November she returned home, and was married at her Father's house. Thence forward she assisted her husband in the Waterville Academy, and again at West Liberty, West Virginia, for the greater part of the time, until her husband's death.

Soon after her marriage Mrs. Bradbury took her younger brother, Boardman Carey, to Waterville, and cared for him till he passed through the Academy and was fitted for College.

years rolls on I shall be far away in the *spirit world*. And what
will be my destiny?

> " When Thou, my Righteous Judge, shall come,
> To take Thy ransome people home,
> Shall I among them stand?"

It is just ten years, to-day, since we came to Houlton to live.
Then you were just as old as Boardy now is. How quickly it has
passed away, and how many changes have taken place in that time !

I must close for I have got to write to Mrs. Clark, Editor of the
Mother's Journal, this evening, and the clock is just striking ten,
now — so good-night, my precious child. May you "abide under
the shadow of the Almighty" is the prayer of

Your affectionate Mother.

HODGDON, Feb. 1, 1856.

MY DEAREST DAUGHTER :

You will see by my date that I am again in Hodgdon. Yes, I
am sitting here, in your Hodgdon home, with the little light stand
drawn up by the fire, and no one else present but your Mother
Bradbury who sits in the rocking chair before the fire reclining
her head on her hand while I am writing. Pa has gone to Orient
to spend the Sabbath, and your Father Bradbury has gone in to
Bro. Outhouse's* to see poor old Mr. Towne,† who lies very low,
and will soon probably leave the shores of time for the boundless
ocean of eternity.

Have you thought, dear Annie, that this is your Mother's birth-

---

*Daniel Outhouse was born in New Brunswick, and came with his parents, at twenty
years of age, to Hodgdon. His Father, John Outhouse, bought land in the South half of
the town, which subsequently came in to Daniel's possession, and remained his home till
his death in 1878.

He experienced religion and was baptised soon after the coming to Hodgdon, having no
thought at the time to be other than a farmer. Eventually he felt that he was called to preach
the gospel, and had a hard struggle to reconcile himself and his wife both to the conviction
of duty. At length light came and he was ordained at Hodgdon, March 4, 1841. He served
that Church as Pastor for one year, then went to Lubec, Washington Co., where he labored
nine years. At the close of that service he came back to his Hodgdon home, and became an
itinerant preacher in this County and the Province. He was an earnest, self denying, successful preacher of the gospel, universally liked, and respected everywhere he went he was
a tower of strength in all the communities. He was a modest, unassuming man, and declined
to become connected with the Missionary Board, on the ground that he was not worthy of
such a position. But he was a sterling man, a safe counsellor; and for the forty-five years
of his Christian living among our people his name was the synonym for all that makes up a
robust, consecrated Christian manliness. He was stricken with the fatal disease on Sunday
morning as he was on the road to his appointment in Ludlow, was carried into a house
near by and died there on the next Tuesday.

†Captain Ebenezer Towne was one of the Second Five Settlers of Hodgdon. H. was

day? Only think! I am fifty-five years old. Just eleven years ago, to-day, we moved into Houlton village; you were then a little girl eleven years old. * * * Now, you are a married woman, and have left your childhood home, and with your own chosen friend have gone to make another happy home for yourselves. O, may

> " Heavenly blessings, without number,
> Gently fall upon your heads!"

We came to Hodgdon, last Sabbath morning, and I have not been home since. Pa went down, Tuesday, on business, and returned Wednesday. We went up to Bro. Foster's Monday, and I stopped up on the Hill till Thursday evening, when we came down to meeting. Pa preached in Houlton Tuesday evening, and on Westford Hill Wednesday eve, and in the Meeting House Thursday evening, so you see his health must be pretty good or he could not do it. I have been about with him nearly all the time since you went away, and he felt quite lonely to go off, alone, down to the Lake but I was too tired to go with him. My health is very good, this winter, but I find it rather too hard to go all the time as poor Pa has to. I had a very good visit on the Hill, spent one whole day at Mr. Adams's. He remains about the same as he has been, for months past, can only get up to have his bed made. * * * I could not finish my letter last evening, and have just set myself down to finish it and to write one to my dear Boardie, but Charles Tarbell has just ridden up, and I have requested him to wait a few moments till I close, so that he can take it to the Post Office for me, as it storms this morning, and I fear that I shall not have another chance to send it, to-day, if I miss this one. Mrs. Whitney lies there just as she did a year ago. They all send love to you. I cannot keep Charlie waiting so I shall have to close. Tell Boardie not to be disappointed, I will write him first, next time. Kiss him hard for his Mother, and tell him I am happy to think he is learning so well.

As ever, your affectionate Mother.

---

born in Topsfield, Essex Co., Mass , June 26, 1773. His wife Mary Pettingill was born in Bridgewater, Plymouth Co , Mass., May 13, 1774.

He got his title in the old militia servic , and moved his family to the Province of New Brunswick in 181?. His trade was that of a mill wright and carpenter. In 1825 he came to Hodgdon, and built the house on the lot of Joseph Kendall, a settler of the First Five. He soon built a house on his own lot near by, and lived there till his later years. His oldest son, Howard P., was the first clerk of the Hodgdon Church, and his youngest daughter was the wife of Rev. D. Outhouse, at whose house he was sick, and where he died, Feb. 22, 1856.

Houlton, May 1, 1856.

My Beloved Daughter:

We have just returned from Hodgdon (after sunset) where we have been almost two weeks.

We sent down last week and got our mail—a letter from you and Boardy—and to-night we called at the P. O. as we came along and found a letter from you and also one from Henry. O how good it is to hear from all our loved ones at once. * * *

I shall not have time, dear Annie, to answer any of *your* letter this evening, but cannot think of going to bed till I have told you what we have been doing at Hodgdon to-day. We have had the pleasantest "May Day" that I ever enjoyed. A number of men and boys met at the meeting house,* this forenoon, and built a very pretty fence around the land belonging to the house, which you know is quite a large piece. About one o'clock they were joined by quite a company of females, old and young, with three or four wagon loads of trees of different kinds, and rose bushes and some other shrubbery, and we have all been at work as busy and cheerful as bees, setting them out, all the afternoon. It seemed like *magic* when we closed, about five, to look at our work and see what a change had taken place since morning.

The trees are all put out for different individuals, some were set out for departed friends and some for absent ones. You and James and Boardy have each a beauty; yours stands next to mine, and Pa's and James's stands right opposite, Boardy's stands next to yours, and your father and mother Bradbury's stand together not far from ours. It was delightful to see each one claiming their tree, and pointing out those they had set for absent friends. Od-

---

*At a business meeting of the Hodgdon Church, held July 8, 1841, Dea. Bradbury was chosen Moderator. On motion it was voted to build a Meeting House, twenty-six by forty-two feet, with posts twelve feet in height. Deas. Bradbury and Jno. White with H. P. Towne were chosen a Building Committee.

The work of construction went forward slowly, for the means at command were not very abundant, and after a year and a half occurs this entry on the records, "Jan. 7, 1843, met for the first time in the new Meeting House."

The house was finished on the outside, as shown in the engraving, but no work at all had been done on the inside except to lay a rough floor, and put up planks on blocks of wood for seats.

No more was accomplished until after the arrival of Mr. Spaulding and family, and through their successful efforts and intercessions the work was brought down to the point of completion to which Mrs. Spaulding makes allusion in this same letter.

Until the completion of the Houlton Meeting House in 1867 this building was the only distinctive Baptist House in the County. In Linneus the Baptists had a third interest in a Union House for some years after 1880.

HODGDON MEETING HOUSE

ber Foster and Zemro Smith and Charley Whitney assisted Pa
(or did the *most*) in setting out yours and mine and Boardy's.

The outside of the meeting house is painted over again, and the
inside is almost done. I wish you could see it. It looks really
neat. The females of our society are deeply interested in making
a carpet for it. I have been helping them spin and double and
twist the warp, and we are going to have the filling made of nicely
cut rags. We expect it will be a very pretty one, and then it will
be our own manufacture, which will add to the interest of it,—
especially as we have no money to purchase one.

Pa wishes me to ask you if you have in your library "Aids to
Devotion," containing Dr. Watts' and Bickersteith's Guide to
Prayer, etc., and another book, "Heart Treasures, or the Furniture
of a Holy Soul," by Rev. Oliver Heywood. He has just got
some new books,* and if these two are not in your library he
wants to send them to you in the box.

We are *so* happy to think our dear little boy is doing so well in
his music and studies, and is a help and comfort to you.

Do kiss him very hard for his father and mother. I can't stop
now to say any more about *any* thing, but will send you another
letter by Monday's mail.

In much love to all, I remain,

Your own affectionate Mother.

Houlton, June 23, 1856.

My Dearest Daughter:

We had a good conference Saturday, and an interesting Sabbath
at Hodgdon, and returned last evening so as to wash to-day and

---

*One of the most important services which Bro. Spaulding rendered to the people of this
section, and the full value of which is above estimation, was constant attention to the work
of circulating good reading in the families wherever he went.

As we call back to mind the familiar forms of the beloved man and his wife, in the little
Concord wagon in summer, in the old fashioned blue sleigh in the winter, both drawn with
becoming gravity by "Old Billy," for it did not seem possible that the little gray horse
could ever have been young, we remember the small trunk which was constantly with them.
From this he drew books for young and old. That trunk was an exhaustless fountain of
intellectual and moral nourishment for almost a generation of people. Nothing like a
book store was kept here till twenty years after he began to work. Over all this region, in
hamlet and lonely cabin in the woods, the tracts, Bibles, and devotional, historical and
biographical books out of this wonderful trunk were spread with a generous hand. It was
not for the money returned that the work was done. His own craving for mental food, and
the widespread needs of the people prompted the faithful and assiduous devotion to this
branch of work.

Thousands of dollars' worth of the best of books were put out by him in the years of his
ministry.

get ready to start, early to-morrow morning, for Presque Isle. Pa has a lecture appointed for to-morrow afternoon about twenty miles from here on the way. Mrs. Clark has been washing for me, and we have had a real party from Hodgdon besides, and a very sociable and agreeable visit.

We went up on Westford Hill, last Friday, and called all round among the folks and spent the night at Bro. Foster's.

Mr. Adams continues to lie upon his bed of languishing yet. All the folks on the Hill send more love to you than I can put in this letter. I don't think of any more Hodgdon news, and I hardly know what is going on in Houlton. Eliphalet Ward died and was buried last week. I wish I was not so tired, I would write to my dear little boy, but I've had a great deal to do since my company went away between four and five o'clock, and I can hardly hold my head up. Tell him I thank him for his large pile of love, and hope it will grow *larger* instead of *smaller*. I must now say good-night and retire, so that I can rise early in the morning and fix off again.

Be assured, dear children, you are all remembered daily, in the prayers of your affectionate.

Father and Mother.

HOULTON, July 9, 1856.

BELOVED CHILDREN :

The long looked for miniatures came this afternoon. Pa went to the Post Office just before tea time and returned in a few minutes with the precious package. We gazed upon your likenesses with joyful hearts and tearful eyes for a long, long time. They look perfectly natural and we *cannot tell* how glad we are to get them. *   *   *

It was a week last evening since we returned from Presque Isle. We stayed at home the next week, but were too tired to write, and we had enough to do besides to keep us quite busy, and the *next day*, Thursday, we went down to the Henderson neighborhood, where Pa had a lecture appointed. We had an interesting meeting and returned home about dark, when Augusta Prince came in and told us that poor little Tommy Blanchard was dead, and that Mrs. B. had sent up for Pa to perform the funeral services on Saturday afternoon. It was our Quarterly Meeting at Hodgdon, Saturday. So we went up Friday, and attended the forenoon meeting Saturday, then came down and attended the funeral, went back again that night, and had a very good meeting Sunday.

We came home from Hodgdon, early Monday morning, and went right up into the Niles neighborhood, where old Mr. Oakes lives, and spent the day in calling upon all the families there; and when we came home we found a man waiting to see Pa to get him to go to Hodgdon the next day to officiate at Mrs. Pollard's funeral. So we went to Hodgdon again yesterday, and returned last evening, and to-day, I have been making me a cap and getting ready to start early in the morning to go over to Woodstock to see Uncle Joseph's folks. We must return to-morrow night, and go to the Lake Friday. So you see how we fly around, and you can imagine how much time I have to write. I could'nt begin this till nearly nine o'clock, and now it is almost ten, and I must get up at *four*, to-morrow morning. * * * We send abundance of love to each and all of you.

Your affectionate Mother.

THE MID-DAY HEAT.

HOULTON, April 8, 1862.

MY VERY DEAR DAUGHTER:

Your welcome letter came to us this evening, and its contents would have surprised us very much if we had'nt been apprised sooner by Henry of your intentions of going back to West Liberty.* Perhaps we may go some day to visit you in your distant home. We should be happy, indeed, to do so, if our Heavenly Father should see fit to bless us with *health, strength,* and means sufficient for so great a journey: but if this privelege is denied us, we have the hope, the glorious hope of meeting in the Heavenly Home, to be separated no more forever.

Pa's face is almost well and his health is tolerably good, but he has not regained his strength; he finds his arduous duties very tiresome, yet we trust he will be gaining in strength and energy. We know, however, that our youthful vigor has passed away and that old age is creeping on: still we hope to live and labor, a little longer, in God's blessed vineyard, for we long to see many souls gathered into the fold of the great and good Shepherd before we go hence to be no more. We had a letter from dear Boardman last week telling us of his safe arrival at Fort Preble.

Now, dear Annie, don't you grieve at all about us. If we were sitting down here, in our desolate home, and mourning over our loneliness you would have some reason to be unhappy about us; but that is not the case. We go from place to place about our missionary labors just as cheerfully as we ever did, and when we

*At the time of these letters Mr. James T. Bradbury with his family and his parents was living at West Liberty, West Virginia. They moved there in 1859, and he was Principal of the Academy till his decease.

The two sons, Henry and Boardman, have enlisted in the Union armies.

come home we call at the Post Office and most always find a letter
or two from dear children or other friends: and then our home
is *so* comfortable we have every thing that heart could wish, and
sweet books to read besides the precious Bible. So when we can
have a few days at home we find it a place of rest and sweet re-
freshment to both body and mind. Our good old *Zion's Advocate* comes every week to cheer us, and also the *New York
Chronicle*, a good religious paper. Dr. Watson of Bangor ordered it sent to us and kindly pays for it himself.

As long as we are able to labor in the vineyard and are as com-
fortably situated as we are we shall feel it our duty to remain at
our post. * * * The Christian people of our village are hold-
ing a union protracted meeting, every afternoon and evening.
They commenced more than a week ago. Pa has attended them
all except on the Sabbath when he had to be away, and I have attended all I could, but I do not go much, evenings, I get so tired.
To-morrow is our State Fast and we have *our* meeting appointed
at the Gilkey neighborhood, and we have promised to spend the
night there.

The people want to do something for us, as Pa preaches there
on the Sabbath, once in four weeks: so they have proposed a
donation visit for us at Mr. Bray's. * * * I will add a line
about the donation after it is over.

Friday, P. M. We had a good meeting at Mr. Bray's yesterday, and the people all seemed very kind. They brought in what
they could, but it is a poor time with them this Spring, and they
were not able to do much, and we were not expecting them to.
But one brought a bunch of stocking yarn, another a pair of stock-
ings for me and a pair for Pa; another a piece of good home-
made flannel to make me a skirt. Others brought some potatoes
and oats, or buckwheat meal, meat, butter, etc. This forenoon
Mr. Daniel Bray came and brought it up with his double team and
a good lot of beautiful straw to fill my beds. The things are such
as we needed and will be a great help to us, so we are not lacking
any good thing. When I see Angelia and Clara I will do your
errand to them.

Millie will find another little picture, and tell him that grand-
pa's and grandma's love comes with it to him, also to little Jimmie
and yourself. Your loving Mother.

HOULTON, March 9, 1863.

DEAREST DAUGHTER:

We got your letter of the 1st of Feb., and I believe I answered it the same evening, while we were at Thomas Bradbury's; so I suppose it has reached you before this time. I think I told you in that that Boardman has gone South to join his regiment. We got a letter from him, last Thursday, dated "Camp near Falmouth, Va., Feb. 24th." He says it is about three miles from Fredericksburg. He says "I am well, but rather tired, as I have no tent, and am obliged to carry logs for my hut, about one and one-half miles, on my back; also my wood for a fire."

Dear Boy! it is quite doubtful if we ever see him again in this world. Quite a number of young men who went into the army from this way will never return, having died of sickness, or been killed in battle, but we do not despair of seeing our dear boy again. We give him up entirely to the providence of God, knowing that whatever He does with him will be right. * * * I have the palpitation of the heart, occasionally, and presume I always shall, while I live, but you know I have got so used to it that I don't mind it much. My health has been very good since I got over my illness, the first of the winter, but Pa and I both, get tired very easily, which we must expect at our age. You may know that I am well, *to-day*, as I have done my washing, (true it was not very large) and washed my floors, and shall have three letters ready for the mail in the morning, besides doing my housework, and had a gentleman to tea in the bargain. Our meeting, yesterday, was in Houlton, in the Niles and Bray Districts, so we were at home last night, and when we are I can have the privilege of washing. *Monday*. Last Sunday, before yesterday, we had our Quarterly Meeting at Hodgdon, commencing the Friday previous. Our meetings were all very interesting, and the blessing of God attended them. They have had meetings every evening since. Bro. Mayo* sent down to-night, for Pa to go up again and

---

*Rev. Leonard Mayo with his family came from Lincolnville, Waldo Co., to Aroostook Co. in the summer of 1857. This movement on his part was suggested to him by Rev. Chas. G. Porter of Bangor, who had been up to Patten, and settlements in the Western part of this Co. Quite a revival had begun, and Bro. Mayo was looked to to carry on the work in that section.

When Bro. Spaulding heard of the matter he wrote Bro. Mayo at once, suggesting that he come to Hodgdon as a more promising field. This letter by some means miscarried and Bro. Mayo first went to Sherman, but in December 1860 he decided to remove to Hodgdon, and take charge of that church and the new one organized at Linneus. None welcomed the

help him, so I think we shall go, Wednesday, if we are well.

We are hoping to form a little Baptist Church here in Houlton, this Spring.* If we succeed I will write you about it. * * * I must say good night, with ever so much love from us both to you all.

Your ever affectionate Father and Mother.

Conclusion of the letter to Mrs. Geo. W. Jones of March 17, 1864:

Yesterday we went thirteen miles up on the Aroostook road to visit a dear, Christian sister, who is fading away with consumption: she had sent for us, two or three times, and we were very

---

new comers more heartily than Bro. and Sister Spaulding. The Hodgdon Church gave a donation soon after Bro. Mayo's arrival, and at that gathering they first met. The Baptist cause was very much strengthened by this new arrangement. The field had outgrown the possibility of being cared for longer by so limited a ministerial force.

The revival alluded to in this letter was the first of many that have constantly attended upon Bro. Mayo's ministry. The ministers present were Bros. Mayo, Spaulding and a licentiate, Bro. Peter McLeod. The meetings continued about three weeks, and fifteen or twenty persons were baptised and joined the church, and among them were the two oldest children of Bro. Mayo.

Bro. Mayo has continued to live in the same home, where they first settled when coming to Hodgdon. He has had a long and useful career as a Pastor in all the towns in this part of the County, and supplemented the work of Bro. Spaulding in a most successful manner.

His six children all experienced religion in the Hodgdon meetings, and are doing useful work in their several places of abode, to-day.

The Baptist Denomination has been most signally blessed by the life work and example of three such men as Bros. Outhouse, Spaulding and Mayo, who have lived so long in these towns.

*A Baptist Church existed " only in name," as Bro. Spaulding wrote to his wife when he first came into the County, so far as Houlton was concerned. An attempt had been made, a few years before, by a few persons, to withdraw from Hodgdon, and make a separate organization for Houlton, but the movement was not endorsed by some of the best members living in the place, and consequently the undertaking soon failed.

No further effort looking to a new centre at Houlton was undertaken until the Spring of 1863.

A sufficient number of new comers were ready to rally to the support of a Baptist Church, and it was found that thirteen persons could be enrolled as the constituent membership.

Eight members of the Hodgdon Church petitioned for dismission to form the new body, and for a council to recognize themselves and associates as the new Church. The church in Linneus was invited to join by its delegates.

In accordance with these requests a Council met in the front room of Bro. Spaulding's house on the afternoon of March 25, and organized with choice of Rev. L. Mayo as Moderator, and Dea. Charles Tarbell, Clerk. Rev. Daniel Outhouse was present, and was invited to sit in the Council.

Rev. R. C. Spaulding and wife presented the Claims of the petitioners and after consideration the Council voted to proceed with services of recognition of them as the First Baptist Church of Houlton. The services were — Singing, Reading of Articles of Faith by Bro. Outhouse, Singing, Prayer by Bro. Outhouse, Address and Right Hand of Fellowship by the Moderator to Rev. R. C. Spaulding for the new Church.

Francis Barnes was then chosen Clerk and Deacon of the Church, after which the Council dissolved.

glad to get a convenient day to go. We found her in a very comfortable and reconciled frame of mind, and so grateful for our visit that we felt truly paid for the tedious ride, the roads being very rough at the present time. To-morrow morning we must start off in an opposite direction and travel thirteen miles, South, on the Calais road, to attend our regular monthly appointments at No. 11, R. 1, and Amity. A conference to-morrow afternoon at No. 11, and one on Sat. afternoon at Amity. Sabbath morning our meeting is at Amity, and in the afternoon at No. 11, about five miles apart. Monday we hope to come home again, if nothing in Providence prevents. There are three or four sick ones now, in different towns (one of them twenty-five miles from here) that we expect, every day, to be called upon to attend the funeral of one or the other. * * *

You and your husband are situated as we are in regard to our *children*, left all alone. The places that our dear ones used to occupy in our own home, *all so desolate* now, but when we hear that any of them are sick or in trouble of any kind we feel it,— it is *our* trouble, but blessed be God! He does not leave us to bear our troubles alone. He sustains us and grants us His supporting and comforting grace. * * *

Henry Martyn belongs to the 1st Regt. Ohio Vol. Heavy Artillery. They have been stationed at Covington, Ky., but were ordered to Knoxville, and are probably there by this time. Boardman was at Fort Preble in Portland for some time this winter, but has been sent to Buffalo, N. Y., on recruiting service: how long he will stay there we do not know.

We hope you will continue to pray for us, dear Brother and Sister Jones, and may God ever bless and prosper you and yours is the sincere prayer of your affectionate

Brother and Sister Spaulding.

HOULTON, Oct. 13, 1865.

DEAR BRO. AND SISTER BRADBURY:

You have no doubt been looking for a letter from us telling you about our Quarterly Meeting, as we promised in our last letter to Annie that we would do so. This is the first opportunity we have had since our meeting closed to fulfil our promise, and *now* we shall have to be brief as possible, because we must go to Belfast, this afternoon.

Well, in the first place, on the morning our meeting began, our good sister, Mary Whitney, came down from Hodgdon to stop with us during the meetings so that she could have a good chance to attend them. That afternoon (Friday) the minister's meeting was at our house, and in the evening the introductory sermon was preached by Bro. Besse of Presque Isle, from John 16 : 7. Saturday morning, met at 10 o'clock. Sermon by Bro. Rigby of Fort Fairfield, text Isaiah 45 : 22. At the close, attended to the business of the Quarterly Meeting. In the evening a sermon by Bro. Powell of Topsfield. Text 1st John 3 : 23. Sabbath morning, met at nine o'clock for prayer. Sermon at half past ten by Bro. Besse, from Matt. 11 : 28-30, then collection was taken for Domestic Missions amounting to nine dollars.

In the afternoon, sermon by Bro. Mayo from 1st Samuel 30 : 6. Evening, a prayer meeting one hour, and then preaching by Bro. Rigby, text, Numbers 10 : 29.

We occupied the Cong. Meeting House and our meetings were all interesting and we hope profitable. The churches were pretty well represented and we had quite a good attendance. Our next Q. M. will meet with the Bap. Church at Presque Isle, on Sat. before the 3d Sunday in Dec. * * *

We have a meeting once in four weeks, on the Sabbath, at Littleton, and next week we expect a baptism there, a Mrs. Briggs. She is an interesting Christian, and a good wife and mother, has a very pleasant family. Our little church here in Houlton is gradually increasing : we have the conference once in four weeks here at our house, and we have a prayer meeting every Friday evening at the Cong. vestry. The female prayer meeting comes on each Wednesday afternoon.

We have not commenced the work of building our Meeting House yet, but hope to be able to make a beginning next Spring.

I must now close as it is time to get ready to go to Belfast. O, may you daily enjoy the comforts of the precious promises, and feel an assurance that you are growing fit for the blessed and glorious mansions above! We think of you, every day, and pray for you, and hope to meet you, by and by, and spend a whole eternity together.

With much love we remain your affectionate Bro. and Sister,

R. C. & J. SPAULDING.

It is a matter of regret that the story of the crowning work of their lives, the building of the Houlton Meeting House, cannot be told in the graphic words of Mrs. Spaulding; but the most careful inquiry has failed to bring to light any letters of that interesting period. Doubtless some were written, though various circumstances tended to hinder as full a measure of correspondence as she had carried on before.

On the one hand Mrs. Bradbury was preparing to leave Virginia, and return home again, and also the arduous labors, with exposures in the past twenty years, were beginning to tell upon them both, but to a greater degree upon Mr. Spaulding than upon his wife.

This made additional care and labor for her in order that they might still keep all their appointments, and, again, the extra strain upon them to carry out what they had undertaken for the Houlton Church so absorbed her energies, that she could not write, from the physical inability to keep up the incessant work.

As soon as a church organization became a fact in Houlton the need of a house of worship was most apparent, and they set about devising the adequate method to meet that need.

They took Council together, but chose to say nothing in public about it. After much of deliberation and prayer they formed their plans and went down to the meetings of the Penobscot Association, in September, 1863, to make a beginning in the way of soliciting funds.

After the meetings they went in to Bangor and visited Mr. Giddings* and his family for a few days. While there Mrs. Spaulding opened up to him the subject which lay so closely to their hearts, and plead for help. He heard the story with attention, thought carefully upon it, consulted with a few of the brethren, some of whom had a personal knowledge of the situation, and as the result, before they left Bangor, the sum of $450.00 was paid

---

*While Miss Jerusha Bryant taught in the Sunday and week day schools in Bangor a little boy, Moses Giddings, was one of her pupils.

Between teacher and scholar, there grew up a mutual esteem and regard. The lad early gave to his teacher good evidence that a work of converting grace had been wrought upon him, and when he was but eleven years of age she declared him worthy to be received by the Church for membership. The cautious conservatism of the church bade him wait until he was older, to the great disappointment of them both.

Change of place and condition of life did not interrupt their well grounded friendship, which, in its steady continuance and abundant fruits, was as honorable to the gifted, missionary wife and the successful business man as it has been conducive to the present success of the Baptist cause in this section.

HOULTON MEETING HOUSE.

by the four men, Arad Thompson, J. C. White, Chapin Humphrey, and Moses Giddings toward the building of the house.

As soon as they reached home they came out to see me, and with delight yet with most serious purpose told the story of their success. "Now we can have a meeting house. Now we must get about the work just as soon as possible."

I was surprised at what they had accomplished, but the more so at the unfolding of their absolute, unquestioning faith in the speedy accomplishment of what they longed for. The hour had come, the instruments had been raised up, and there was money enough to begin with.

In the month of February following, the lot of land was bought for $250.00, and the balance was deposited in Bangor. Despite the earnest faith of the good man and his wife the prospect, to ordinary persons, for immediate success in the enterprise was not very promising. The church was small in numbers, weak in a money point of view, and had no large body of sympathizers in the community.

A whole year went by without further opportunity for progress, and their only encouragement rested in their unwavering confidence of ultimate success. In March, 1865, a small brow of choice lumber, at No. 11, was bought at a fair price with the balance of the money on hand.

These logs were driven to the Hodgdon millpond, and remained there till the next Fall. The door to further advancement did not open. It did not seem expedient to seek further aid until the word had come to go forward at Houlton. Bro. Spaulding and his wife were narrowed up to prayer and waiting, for month after month.

As we now recall those days, the manner of life of that godly couple, in their home, comes back most forcibly to view. The conference meetings and all the more formal interviews were held in the front room, but the closet of prayer in that house, really, was the kitchen, in its spotless condition of neatness and exact arrangement.

A person might call many times and think that nothing was ever moved out of place in that room. The table always stood between the windows with a chair at each end, the stove was opposite, well back in the old fashioned fireplace, and two or three other chairs for callers were near by.

They invariably sat in the same places, he to rest his right arm on the table, and she her left, as they talked, counselled and advised with their visitors. Here was the seat of the wonderous power which worked through them. No one who entered that closet of devotion but felt its influence upon them. Would that the faithful camera could reproduce that scene!

It was my privilege and duty to enter that inner shrine, many times, under all kinds of conditions of church exigencies, and invariable the accompaniment on their part was earnest prayer on bended knee.

In the winter of 1865-66 an affectual door for advancement was opened, and to the inexpressible satisfaction of these watchmen on the walls we all felt that the word had come, "Go forward."

When the design for the house had been settled upon the estimated cost of the structure exceeded the value of unincumbered property which was in the possession of the members of the church.

The contracts were let for the various parts of the work early in the season of 1866. Pledges of aid had been obtained in Bangor, Portland, and other places. While the work of construction went on from week to week, prayer and planning about ways and means went on in that closet kitchen. On one occasion, as I called there, Mrs. Spaulding said to me, "We will get all the shingles you will need without the use of any money." They went to their friends in the Niles neighborhood and vicinity, and coaxed and urged the men there to help to that extent. Such pleading could not be withstood, and right in the month of June the brethren and their friends went into the swamps, and cut and carried out on their shoulders the bolts of cedar which they then made into the shingles.

By such efforts the roof was covered, and so well that the same shingles are doing duty on that roof to-day.

The Fourth of July brought the severest test of faith and works which was met with in that year. The two Portland churches had subscribed liberally in our aid, and payments from them were relied upon to meet the midsummer bills of wages and supplies. The great fire which so cruelly ravaged that city, on that day, destroyed the possibility of a single dollar reaching us from the

First Church, and a feeling of blank dismay settled down upon all of us except two.

Utterly at my wits ends to devise a method of extrication for us, and fearing a complete stoppage of the work, I went almost instinctively up the street to call at that little inner room. While I could well know there was not money in any amount, there, yet the way of relief would be devised by them if it were to come at all. Bro. Spaulding and his wife were sitting in their accustomed seats when I entered the room, and they told me they had been praying for the needed wisdom to guide them aright in this crisis.

After we had talked over the situation in all its bearings they said with earnestness and with the most complete self-abnegation, "The work on the Meeting House must not stop. We will mortgage our house, and give you the money to pay the men."

It seemed best to let the brethren in Bangor know what they purposed to do, and they sent word back immediately not to allow that home to be mortgaged, and they would find a way to keep the work along.

After that experience it was a needless thing to question the ultimate issue of the undertaking. As the work neared completion the pressure for means followed hard after us. We had enough to go on with, but nothing in advance. It became a serious question how to provide for the purchase of the pulpit furniture. But Mrs. Spaulding was ready for the emergency.

"We women will find that furniture," and when needed the pieces were all in place and paid for. The pulpit Bible was a gift from a sister of Mrs. Spaulding.

With a pulpit prepared, who should occupy it, was a question which was not lost sight of. Mr. Spaulding had said, "It is not my place and I shall not go into it." His was the place of the forerunner, and his prayer was, day by day, "Send us a man of Thine own choosing, O Lord." The prayer was answered in a manner we did not look for. Rev. Chas. G. Porter had been the beloved and successful pastor of the Second Baptist Church in Bangor for more than twenty years, when his health began to fail, and it seemed to all appearance that his days of active labor were about over. He resigned his charge, another man stepped into that place and it was very uncertain whether he would take up work again. The Penobscot Association met in 1866 at Oldtown, where Bro. Porter was present, and entered into the discussions, and learned of the prospects in Houlton. The next day, I met him in the store of B. F. Bradbury, in Bangor, and grasping my hand with earnestness he said, "Barnes, when you get that Meeting House ready, I am coming up to preach the dedication sermon for you."

With the hour came the man, to renew his health in a measure, and do great and lasting work in his Master's vineyard.

In the last days of January 1867, in the midst of drifting snows, which caused the stage to upset twice in the ride of the first day, Bro. Porter and his wife came to Houlton. It is to be doubted if, in all the Baptist ministry of the State at that time, there was another man so well fitted for the work before him as Mr. Porter was. He was to take the work from the hands of Mr. and Mrs. Spaulding, with care that there should be no backward movement, to build up the Houlton interest, and to strengthen the Denomination in the County at large.

The last significant scene now transpired in the closet kitchen of the Spaulding home.

It was known on what day Bro. Porter expected to arrive in Houlton, and they agreed to be at home to meet him. After the arrival of the stage, and the travelers had got warmed, I said to him that Mr. and Mrs. Spaulding were anxious to see him. We soon reached the house, entered the door without stopping to knock, and passed through the long passageway to the kitchen into which Bro. Porter stepped first. With his quick nervous step, and with a genial smile upon his face, he passed over to where Mr. Spaulding stood, and shook his hand saying, "Bro. Spaulding, I am glad to see you here." "Bro. Porter, I am thankful to greet you here in my home," was the response. Then he turned and saluted Mrs. Spaulding, but her feelings were too deep for words. The tears filled her eyes as she looked upon the man before her, realized how much had been accomplished, and saw in Bro. Porter, the Denomination come to take up the work to which their lives had been devoted.

After the work.

THE SUNSET HOUR.

Bro. Spaulding was laid aside from the sphere of active life for quite a number of years before he was summoned to his reward. He was tenderly cared for by his devoted wife, and the circle of ministering friends.

On Wednesday, Sept. 1st, 1880, the end came, and it was a peaceful close to a long life. On Friday following, the funeral services were held at his house, and were conducted by Rev. Isaiah Record,* Pastor of the Baptist Church.

On the following Sunday Evening, to a large audience which filled the Meeting House to overflowing, Bro. Record delivered the memorial discourse, which was afterward repeated before the Penobscot Association, at Bangor, then printed in the *Advocate*, and an abstract is also found in the Convention Minutes for that year.

Although Bro. Record had known him, personally, only four years, and in all of this time he was a confirmed invalid, nevertheless, owing to a peculiar identity of spiritual endowment, Pastor Record had fully appreciated the work and self-sacrifice of this pioneer who had preceeded him; and his discourse was filled with most tender and heartfelt tributes to the worth of the Father in Israel.

The text chosen was Acts, 13: 36. "For David, after he had served his own generation by the will of God, fell on sleep."

The earlier portion of the discourse was a statement of the facts of Mr. Spaulding's career, as found in the autobiographical

*Isaiah Record, born in Livermore, Androscoggin County, Me., 1835. W. C. 1862. Degree of A. M., 1870. Newton Theolog. Seminary, 1869. Pastor, Turner, Me., 1869-76. Houlton, 1876-83. Trustee Houlton Academy, 1878-83. Died, Houlton, Me., March 14, 1883.

sketch. The speaker then summed up in the following forcible words:

"He gathered out the stones, prepared the way for the victorious coming of the Lord, strengthened the weak, and organized the scattered children of our King into churches. And then he nourished these churches with all the care and patience which the fondest parents exercise toward their children."

After this came the lessons to be drawn from his life, and as we now read the touching and graceful words of the preacher, who so soon followed his subject into the silent land, we realize that, all unconsciously, he narrated those very qualities of manliness, humility, self-sacrifice, consecration, and trust, which although displayed under the changed conditions yet make the name and memory of Isaiah Record most tenderly cherished by the people of Houlton.

"Now what was it that enabled Bro. Spaulding to accomplish so much? First, he was a true man. No one ever distrusted him, or had cause to do so. He was just what he professed to be, a man of God, walking in all His commandments blameless. Does any one think this is a small matter, or one so common as not to deserve attention? Doubtless there are many good men, many godly. But there are not so many as we could wish whose goodness and piety are so transparent as were Bro. Spaulding's. Men of all beliefs, and no beliefs, took it for granted that he was a good and pious man; that he was worthy of their confidence and esteem. He was able, therefore, to work with ease and power that could not have been possible had it been otherwise.

He often felt his own unworthiness very deeply in the sight of God, but he never had cause to doubt that he was trusted and loved by his brethren, and by the people generally who knew him. His correct and devout life gave great force to his sermons and exhortations.

It is also true that few men have devoted themselves more entirely to the work of the gospel. He was not able, situated as he was, to spend so much labor on pulpit preparations as he desired. But still his work was always connected, in some way, with the furtherance of the gospel.

He gave but little time or thought to secular employments. He was too much filled and possessed by the theme, Jesus Christ and Him crucified, ever to be turned aside from his life's work. I do not mean by this that Bro. Spaulding was only anxious for the conversion of men, or that he considered it his only mission to gather them into churches. Perhaps there are very few preachers who are wiser than he was in building men up in righteousness.

Again few men ever denied themselves more for Christ's sake than he did. If he had followed his natural taste he would have sought a field of labor where he would have time for reading and study instead of coming into a new country, and engaging in pioneer work.

He loved books and accumulated a large library, hoping some time, perhaps in the debility of old age, to have time to learn what it contained. But his employment afforded him little leisure for reading. He could only snatch an occasional hour from his active duties for reading. But he submitted cheerfully to such privations in order that he might do his Master's work.

He never allowed personal considerations to stand in the way of usefulness. This would be very apparent to all, if we knew how little money he received during the period of his active labors, and how much he gave away. Our brother stated, in a letter to the Penobscot Association, after he had been here twenty-one years, that he had put in circulation $2800 worth of religious reading. Of course not all this amount came out of his own pocket. Some of the books were paid for by those who received them. But many of them he furnished gratis. The Missionary Board gave him a stipulated sum of money each year. But beyond this his support was fragmentary and precarious. Some of it he received in produce, and a little he received in money from those who were able to pay. He was compelled to practice the strictest economy in order to meet the expenses of his family, yet he always found something to give to the needy, and to all our benevolent organizations. He frequently took from his own house a portion of what he had laid by for his family and carried it away to those whom he thought needed it more. He could not look upon the hungry and distressed without doing what he could for their relief, no matter how great the sacrifice to himself.

Again his trust in God was full and entire. However dark the way appeared he never seemed to doubt for a moment the ultimate success of the gospel. He fully believed that it was the power of God unto salvation.

He labored as a pioneer, when there were few to help him, and little that could be seen affording hope save to the eye of faith. And his faith resulted in victory.

When he came to this county the only Baptist Church was in Hodgdon. But before he was laid aside by infirmities, he assisted in organizing churches in Linneus, in Houlton, in Amity and Cary, in Smyrna, in Ludlow, in Orient, and in New Limerick. His labors and prayers have materially aided in whatever has been accomplished by Baptists in this whole region.

There was a strong, yet tender, tie of sympathy which drew him toward others and drew others toward him. Men felt the power of his generous and loving heart which always beat so true toward them, and hence they heeded his words and advice.

It should be added that he had an abounding charity. He saw the good side of every person he met instead of the bad. If he saw anything that was not right in others it never seemed to impress itself on his mind. Only the good traits remained in his memory. It may also be truly said that he never harbored a feeling of jealousy toward any of his brethren. Indeed, I doubt, whether such a feeling ever entered his heart.

Another trait in his character, closely connected with that which has just been mentioned was his appreciation of benefits received. He and his wife have always felt just as grateful for every favor received as if they had never done anything for their fellow creatures. They have never for a moment thought that the world owed them a living, and hence was under obligation to support them.

Brother Spaulding bore the heavy cross laid upon him, in his last years, without murmuring and with true Christian resignation. At times, too, joy filled his heart, and light from the New Jerusalem shone upon him. And at last he fell peacefully asleep in Jesus.

He served his generation, and he has heard the welcome plaudit from the lips of the Master, "Well done, good and faithful servant!"

The Penobscot Association met with the First Baptist Church of Bangor, on the Tuesday following the death of Bro. Spaulding, and yielding to the urgent wishes of her friends, Mrs. Spaulding went once more, and for the last time, to the meetings, of which, for so many years, she and her husband had been a large part. The Minutes of that year contain touching allusions to the presence of this aged servant of God. Rev. F. T. Hazlewood offered the following: "Whereas, God in His love has removed from our care our beloved Bro. Spaulding, and in place of the annual letter from him and his devoted wife has given us the presence of the widowed companion; therefore this Association by rising vote does now express its sense of loss in the death of our Brother, and its delight still to reverence and care for the living." Mrs. Spaulding briefly responded, expressing her gratitude for the respect and esteem manifested for her husband and herself, indicated by the vote just passed, and also for the kind personal attention and sympathy received from the brothers and sisters during the session. The final line of the record is, "the presence of Sister Spaulding, so recently bereaved, added much to the interest of the occasion."

After her return she continued to live in the old home with her daughter, and in the enjoyment of a fair degree of health was able to attend the Sunday services until almost the time of her last sickness.

HOULTON, June 30, 1881.

DEAR BRO. GIDDINGS:

Your kind letter with your picture was very welcome and acceptable, and you will please accept my warmest thanks. It is very pleasing and gratifying to be so long and so kindly remembered by one who, in his boyhood, was a loved pupil in my school, and I can truly say that your friendship and beneficence have been like an unfailing spring to me in all these years that I have lived in Aroostook County. * * *

I should have made a longer visit in Bangor but my physical strength was failing me so much that I thought it best to come home while I could, and I have now got nicely rested and am feeling that my journey was a benefit to my health after all. I am now enjoying, in retrospect, the very interesting visits with my friends wherever I went.

Our Church here are looking forward with great interest to our Association and hope to see a large delegation from all the churches. I trust we shall all be praying that the Lord will meet with us of a truth and pour us out a blessing so that we shall receive a spiritual refreshing from His presence, and be prepared and strengthened for more earnest self-sacrificing work in His vineyard.

Hoping at that time to see you and Mrs. Giddings, and a good many more of our Bangor friends, I am, with kindest regards,

Yours very sincerely,

J. SPAULDING.

HOULTON, April 29, 1883.

MY DEAR NIECES:

Since your dear Mother died I have been waiting to feel well enough to write you a letter, not to mourn with you, for I can truly say I feel more like *rejoicing* that she has been called, after her long and eventful life here below, to enter upon that eternal life of joy and blessedness which Jesus promised to His believing followers, and O, how sweet must be her rest in the presence of the dear Saviour, where sin and sorrow can no more molest or make her afraid! She was called to pass through many afflictions here which sometimes seemed heavier than she could bear, but how different they will look to her now. When they come to her memory, she will feel that they were "light afflictions" and were blessings to bring her nearer to Jesus and His love.

My health has been so poor the past winter that I have often thought I should be the first one of us four sisters to leave the scenes of earth; but for some wise purpose God is sparing my poor life a little longer, and O, that the remnant of my days may be spent to His honor and glory! My health now is much better, but still I am so weak that every little effort tires me. This has been a beautiful day, and I had the privilege of going to church, this forenoon, by leaning on Jimmie's arm as I cannot walk very straight alone. A Presbyterian minister preached for us to-day, but not being used to his voice, and being so hard of hearing, I did not understand much of the sermon. We sadly miss our dear good minister, but we hope and pray that God may not leave us, but in His good time send us one after His own heart to break unto us the bread of life.

Monday, A. M. Having my morning's work done up and my pen in hand I thought to write a little more, but I have some business to attend to, that must not be put off, in regard to my good paper the *Zion's Advocate* which will take the rest of the day. I shall have to say good by for this time, with ever so much love from us all to each of you, and to any good friends who may inquire for us.

Your loving Aunt,

J. SPAULDING.

HOULTON, Jan. 1, 1884.

MY DEAR MRS. GIDDINGS:

Your kind letter with the generous present enclosed was most gratefully received by me last night, and will you and each of the kind donors please accept my earnest thanks for the same, and also for the good wishes expressed. May God abundantly bless and reward! Truly the Lord's mercies to me are wonderful, and in view of my great unworthiness to receive them my spirit is humbled within me. Bless the Lord, Oh, my soul and forget not all his benefits!

I congratulate you and your husband on the addition of two beautiful grandchildren to your number of dear ones; but above all for the conversion of your precious younger daughter. May she prove to be a shining light to all around her, living daily to the honor and glory of God and doing good.

I have no doubt but that our church and society had the sympathy and prayers of all the churches in our Association in our great sorrow at the loss to us of our good Pastor Record. * * *

It is growing dark and I must close with much love and many good wishes for your dear family, the church, and the Sabbath school of which you are all members; and may God bless you all is the earnest prayer of your sister in Christ,

JERUSHA SPAULDING.

The above letter was nearly the last one which Mrs. Spaulding ever wrote, for in April following her strength entirely failed, and after a short period of sickness, on May 3, 1884, she passed on to her reward.

No more fitting eulogy on the blended lives of these dear persons could be given than is contained in the following reminiscences of two of their "children in the Lord," Miss Hattie T. Mayo of Hodgdon, and Mrs. Jenny E. Seamans of Cary.

Miss Mayo writes:

I remember many times in my childhood when we had the pleasure of having Mr. and Mrs. Spaulding in our home, a pleasure that was anticipated for hours before they came.

Saturday morning, my brothers would say, "We will watch for their team, and invite them to stay to dinner," a proposal to which all the family were agreed, and if some parts of the Saturday's work which fell to my hands were a little irksome the task was suddenly lightened when my Mother said, "Mrs. Spaulding would like to see the work nicely done"; that was sure to have the desired effect.

When they came they always seemed glad to see every member of the family, no one being overlooked in their kindly greeting.

Mrs. Spaulding always noticed what we were doing and would say to my sisters, "Well I should enjoy that work," or, "I should like to read" such a book referring to something they had been reading.

In speaking of others, she invariably referred to their virtues and seemed quite unconscious of their faults. "I always loved them" often fell from her lips and "thinketh no evil" is in my mind closely connected with her memory.

I cannot remember that Mrs. Spaulding ever spoke to me personally on the subject of religion, but her *life* spoke *constantly* for Christ, and in no way was it more manifest to me than in her loving thoughtfulness and interest in all classes of people.

Once a year Mr. Spaulding brought to us "The Baptist Almanac," which was to me a library in itself: there I first read of Judson and Bunyan and other noted men.

I have in my possession a book entitled "The Lighted Way" given to me when a child by Mr. Spaulding. I appreciated the pretty red cover before I opened it, then was pleased with it because of the giver, and afterward learned to prize it because of its lessons.

Mrs. Seamans writes:

I well remember how pleased we used to be when Mr. and Mrs. Spaulding came to this neighborhood, once in four weeks, during the first years that we lived in the place. Their coming was like "sunshine in a dark place" to us. Their manner of living their religion was such that children had no fear of them, but looked upon their visits as the greatest possible cause for enjoyment.

They were watchful for opportunities to do good, in speaking a word to a child, by reading some interesting story, or relating some incident of interest or profit.

Mrs. Spaulding knew just how to adapt herself to any circumstance in which she might be placed, and make it a chance to do good. She would visit the poorest homes and by her pleasant manner make herself so welcome that those whom she visited would feel at ease and could thoroughly enjoy her visit.

Her memory remains a constant benediction. How well I recall when, as I returned to my desolate home after the burial of my husband she took me in her arms and whispered to me, "Jenny, you must lean hard upon Jesus." How those words comforted and helped me! She did not tell me it was wrong to mourn and that I must become reconciled to the will of God. She knew I was not unreconciled, even though I mourned, and she knew just what was the needed word of comfort.

Dear precious saint! my eyes fill with tears as I write of her! Eternity alone will reveal the good which Mr. and Mrs. Spaulding did in their lives. Their labors in the cause of Christ were self-denying and faithful. The watch care they exercised over these little churches, was vigilant and unremitting. They cherished them as their own children, and loved them unto death.

In the long years of pain and helplessness through which Mr. Spaulding was called to pass, how faithful and constant was the care which Mrs. Spaulding gave to him, never seeming to think of herself, if she could only be spared to minister to him!

I never shall forget how deeply impressed I was with the exhibition of the love which everybody felt toward her, as I tarried in her home during the days between her death and burial.

So many came to the house to look at her as she lay in her last sleep. Little children rapped at the door, and when I opened it, would say, "We want to see Mrs. Spaulding." Colored people whom she had befriended, poor people whom she had helped, came and looked at her with tears in their eyes. More than one exclaimed " She was always so good to me."